D

RDED

D1326625

For Brian Farran,
who cares about these matters, J.M.

For Nick, S.T.

A Lothian Children's Book

Published in Australia and New Zealand
by Hachette Australia Pty Ltd
Level 17, 207 Kent Street, Sydney NSW 2000
www.hachettechildrens.com.au

Text copyright © Jomden Pty Ltd 1998
Illustrations copyright © Shaun Tan 1998

First published 1998
Reprinted 1998, 1999, 2001, 2003, 2005
Large edition first published 2008
Reprinted 2009, 2010 (twice), 2011, 2012

Paperback edition first published 2000
Reprinted 2001, 2003 (twice), 2004, 2005, 2006, 2007, 2008
This large paperback edition first published 2008
Reprinted 2009 (three times), 2010 (twice), 2011 (twice), 2012 (twice), 2013 (twice),
2014 (three times), 2015, 2016

This book is copyright. Apart from any fair dealing for the purposes of
private study, research, criticism or review permitted under the *Copyright Act*
1968, no part may be stored or reproduced by any process without prior
written permission. Enquiries should be made to the publisher.

National Library of Australia
Cataloguing-in-Publication data:

Marsden, John, 1950– .
   The Rabbits.
   ISBN 978 0 7344 1078 8 (hbk.)
   ISBN 978 0 7344 1136 5 (pbk.)
   I. Tan, Shaun. II Title.
A823.3

Designed by Shaun Tan
Cover design by Tony Gilevski
Colour reproduction by Chroma Graphics, Singapore
Printed in China by Toppan Leefung Printing Limited

THE RABBITS

John Marsden & Shaun Tan

LOTHIAN
Children's Books

THE RABBITS CAME
MANY GRANDPARENTS AGO.

AT FIRST WE DIDN'T KNOW WHAT TO THINK. THEY LOOKED A BIT LIKE US

THERE WEREN'T MANY OF THEM. SOME WERE FRIENDLY.

BUT OUR OLD PEOPLE WARNED US:

BE CAREFUL.

THEY WON'T UNDERSTAND THE RIGHT WAYS.

THEY ONLY KNOW THEIR OWN COUNTRY.

MORE RABBiTS CaMe....

THEY CAME BY WATER.

WE COULDN'T UNDERSTAND THE WAY THEY TALKED.

THEY BROUGHT NEW FOOD, AND THEY BROUGHT OTHER ANIMALS.

WE LIKED SOME OF THE FOOD AND WE LIKED SOME OF THE ANIMALS.

BUT SOME OF THE FOOD

MADE US SICK

AND SOME OF THE ANIMALS SCARED US.

THE RaBBiTS SPREAD ACROSS THE COUNTRY.

NO MOUNTAIN COULD STOP THEM; NO DESERT, NO RIVER.

STILL MORE OF THEM CAME.

SOMETIMES WE HAD FIGHTS,

BUT THERE WERE TOO MANY RABBITS.

They ate our grass.

They chopped down our trees and scared away our friends...

RaBBiTS, RaBBiTS, RaBBiTS.
MiLLiONS AND MiLLiONS OF RaBBiTS.
EVERYWHERE WE LOOK THERE ARE RaBBiTS.

The Land is BARE and BROWN and The WIND BLOWS EMPTY across the Plains.

Where is the rich, dark earth,
brown and moist?
Where is the smell of rain
dripping from the gum trees?

WHERE ARE THE GREAT BILLABONGS
ALIVE WITH LONG-LEGGED BIRDS?

WHO WILL SAVE US FROM THE RABBITS?